Phonics Friends

Victor Moves
The Sound of **V**

By Joanne Meier and Cecilia Minden

The **Child's World**

3 1257 01659 1447

Published in the United States of America
by The Child's World®
PO Box 326
Chanhassen, MN 55317-0326
800-599-READ
www.childsworld.com

A special thank you to the Lumsden family for providing the modeling for this book.

The Child's World®: Mary Berendes, Publishing Director

Editorial Directions, Inc.: E. Russell Primm, Editorial Director and Project Editor; Katie Marsico, Associate Editor; Judith Shiffer, Associate Editor and School Media Specialist; Linda S. Koutris, Photo Researcher and Selector

The Design Lab: Kathleen Petelinsek, Design and Page Production

Photographs ©: Photo setting and photography by Romie and Alice Flanagan/Flanagan Publishing Services: cover, 4, 10, 20; Corbis/Bohemian Nomad Picturemakers/Kevin R. Morris: 12; Corbis/Ron Watts: 14; Corbis/Walter Hodges: 16; Getty Images/Brand X/SW Productions: 8; Getty Images/FoodPix/Burke/Triolo Productions: 6; Getty Images/The Image Bank/Yellow Dog Productions: 18.

Library of Congress Cataloging-in-Publication Data
Meier, Joanne D.
  Victor moves : the sound of V / by Joanne Meier and Cecilia Minden.
    p. cm. — (Phonics friends)
  Summary: Simple text featuring the sound of the letter "v" describes Victor's move to a new house.
  ISBN 1-59296-307-2 (library bound : alk. paper)
  [1. English language—Phonetics. 2. Reading.] I. Minden, Cecilia. II. Title. III. Series.
  PZ7.M5148Vi 2004
  [E]—dc22   2004003542

Note to parents and educators:

The Child's World® has created Phonics Friends with the goal of exposing children to engaging stories and pictures that assist in phonics development. The books in the series will help children learn the relationships between the letters of written language and the individual sounds of spoken language. This contact helps children learn to use these relationships to read and write words.

The books in this series follow a similar format. An introductory page, to be read by an adult, introduces the child to the phonics feature, or sound, that will be highlighted in the book. Read this page to the child, stressing the phonic feature. Help the student learn how to form the sound with her mouth. The Phonics Friends story and engaging photographs follow the introduction. At the end of the story, word lists categorize the feature words into their phonic element. Additional information on using these lists is on The Child's World® Web site listed at the top of this page.

Each book in this series has been carefully written to meet specific readability requirements. Close attention has been paid to elements such as word count, sentence length, and vocabulary. Readability formulas measure the ease with which the text can be read and understood. Each Phonics Friends book has been analyzed using the Spache readability formula. For more information on this formula, as well as the levels for each of the books in this series please visit The Child's World® Web site.

Reading research suggests that systematic phonics instruction can greatly improve students' word recognition, spelling, and comprehension skills. The Phonics Friends series assists in the teaching of phonics by providing students with important opportunities to apply their knowledge of phonics as they read words, sentences, and text.

This is the letter *v.*

In this book, you will read words that have the *v* sound as in:

very, moving, seven, and *visit.*

Victor is very happy!

He is moving to a new house.

It is seven hours away.

Victor will make new friends.

He can also visit his old friends.

It is fun to move.

Victor puts every toy in a box.

The movers put every box in the van. They drive the van to the new house.

Victor and his mother ride

in their car.

Victor waves to the big trucks.

Some of the drivers wave back.

Victor sees the new house.

It is very big. He loves it!

Victor gives his mother

a big grin. He never wants

to move again!

Fun Facts

Vans come in all sizes. Some vans are the perfect size for a family. Does your family have a van? Some vans need to be larger to carry mail or packages. Vans carrying food to restaurants and grocery stores can be very large. A moving van is one of the largest vans on the road. Do you know how much a moving van weighs when it is full of furniture and boxes? It can weigh about 10,000 pounds (4,536 kilograms)!

Imagine moving west in a covered wagon. Moving then was much different than it is today. Most people moved in small farm wagons because they were much easier to maneuver. Children could take only one or two small toys. Most of the space in the wagon was taken up by clothing and food. A family of four needed 1,000 pounds (454 kg) of food to survive the trip from the East to Oregon or California.

Activity

Building a Playhouse with Moving Boxes

Do you think boxes are just for moving or storing things? Use moving boxes to construct a playhouse. You can even put two or three boxes together to make a playhouse with more than one room. Ask a parent to help you if you need to work with scissors to cut the cardboard. When you are finished making your playhouse, decorate it with crayons or markers.

To Learn More

Books
About the Sound of V
Ballard, Peg. *Vets: The Sound of V*. Chanhassen, Minn.: The Child's World, 2000.

About Moving
Brown, Marc. *Arthur's Teacher Moves In*. Boston, Mass.: Little, Brown, 2000.
Smith, Lane. *The Happy Hocky Family Moves to the Country*. New York: Viking, 2003.
Wells, Rosemary, and Susan Jeffers (illustrator). *McDuff Moves In*. New York: Hyperion Books for Children, 1997.

About Vans
Ernst, Lisa Campbell. *This is the Van That Dad Cleaned*. New York: Simon and Schuster Books for Young Readers, 2005.
Maestro, Betsy, and Giulio Maestro (illustrator). *Delivery Van: Words for Town and Country*. New York: Clarion Books, 1990.
McKay, Sandy, and Meredith Johnson (illustrator). *The Big Tan Van*. San Francisco: Treasure Bay, 2001.

Web Sites
Visit our home page for lots of links about the Sound of V:
http://www.childsworld.com/links.html

Note to Parents, Teachers, and Librarians: We routinely check our Web links to make sure they're safe, active sites—so encourage your readers to check them out!

V Feature Words

Proper Names

Victor

Feature Words in Initial Position

van

very

visit

Feature Words in Medial Position

drive

driver

every

give

love

move

mover

moving

never

seven

wave

About the Authors

Joanne Meier, PhD, has worked as an elementary school teacher and university professor. She earned her BA in early childhood education from the University of South Carolina, and her MEd and PhD in education from the University of Virginia. She currently works as a literacy consultant for schools and private organizations. Joanne Meier lives with her husband Eric, and spends most of her time chasing her two daughters, Kella and Erin, and her two cats, Sam and Gilly, in Charlottesville, Virginia.

Cecilia Minden, PhD, directs the Language and Literacy Program at the Harvard Graduate School of Education. She is a reading specialist with classroom and administrative experience in grades K–12. She earned her PhD in reading education from the University of Virginia. Cecilia and her husband Dave Cupp enjoy sharing their love of reading with their granddaughter Chelsea.